THE URBAN EROTICA
FAIRY TALE COLLECTION

I0583943

Goldie and her
Three Beards

THE URBAN EROTICA
FAIRY TALE COLLECTION

Goldie and her Three Beards

HONEY CUMMINGS

DEDICATION

For all those who utilize all those amazing
apps during those tender
looking-for-love times!

THE DILEMMA

Valentine's Day was only two days away and Goldie didn't even have a date, let alone a boyfriend.

Pulling a lock of golden hair over her shoulder, she scoffed. The new golden tan and near professional level makeup did nothing, and the sexy lingerie now lay abandoned in her top drawer. Nothing seemed to get her the attention she wanted from the opposite sex. Around the office, her coworkers chattered about their dinner plans, their dates, and their bedroom plans.

She could still hear Kyle's words the week before Christmas. *It's not you, it's me.*

What a lame excuse. Who are you fooling, Kyle? We both know you picked that fight to avoid buying me anything. Guess who now has a new Apple Watch? Merry Christmas to me!

"Goldie." DeeDee, her cubicle mate, popped her head over the partition wall like a noisy neighbor. "What plans do you have for V-day?"

"Nada." Goldie leaned back in her office chair, spinning slow and aimless. "I've no plans nor a no man, DeeDee. This sucks."

She disappeared, then reappeared in the cubicle doorway. "You've had a whole month to figure something out. What's wrong?"

"I don't know. No one feels... just right." She stopped spinning and collapsed onto her desk, hiding her face. "It's like being hungry and not knowing what to eat."

DeeDee laughed. "You know what this means, right?"

Goldie groaned and peeked over her arm. "I don't know, DeeDee." *It couldn't be anything good.*

DeeDee pulled out her phone and wiggled it. "Time to download Sinder and find yourself a date!"

Goldie stared at the drop-down ceiling. DeeDee had recommended the top dating app in the country before she met Kyle, even after Kyle ended their relationship.

She grabbed her cell phone and looked up the app, her finger hovering over the download button. She had made it this far without using this monstrosity of an idea, but her desire for companionship, on Valentine's Day placed too much pressure on her. *Why can't cupid just spare a minute and help me out?*

"It's either the app or BOB." DeeDee leaned over her shoulder. "Take your pick. You're running out of options, girlie."

"Bob?" Goldie furrowed her brow. "Who the hell is that?"

DeeDee's smirked, then her breath tickled Goldie's ear. "Battery Operated Boyfriend."

Groaning, Goldie hit download. "Nope."

"Oh, come on." DeeDee laughed, leaning on the desk. "Don't discredit a night with Bob."

"I wouldn't if he could do it for me." Her face flushed, watching the download bar grow.

Unlike her friends, sex toys like pocket rockets, vibrators, and dildos just didn't satisfy the same. Sure, they worked in a pinch when she couldn't temper her horny desires, but this wasn't how she wanted to spend her Valentine's Day! She wanted the real thing, bent over and pounded until she came. Or a man's lips against her pussy while his beard added pleasure between her thighs.

The app loaded and launched. She created an account and was immediately bombarded with what felt like fifty billion questions in the form of survey-styled questionnaire. Each question designed to impress and attract, to recommend the best match for the type of man (or woman if she wanted) for hooking up and

4

dating. She glared at the profile section, the idea of typing it via her phone was far too annoying.

"I'll finish signing up tonight," Goldie declared, closing the app.

"Boo. I wanted to watch you answer some of those questions." DeeDee twisted her lips, then shrugged. "Remember, swipe left for no and right for... just right."

With that, DeeDee winked and left.

Goldie rolled to her computer to finish her workday. Every so often, she'd glance at the phone, fear and excitement pushing her work task back into her mind. *What on earth have I gotten myself into?*

THE SETUP

Pouring deep red wine into a glass, Goldie settled on the couch with her laptop. She steeled herself, going through and filling out all the mandatory information. It felt strange creating a sultry bio in hopes of spicing up her dull, ordinary life. Sure, she had hobbies, but the last time she physically visited a beach had been well over a year.

She froze. *Shit.* The last thing she needed was a photo. *Should I use an old one? No, that's a terrible idea. Maybe I should...*

Abandoning the wine glass and laptop on the end table, she marched into her bathroom. Pulling out every makeup bag and hair product she owned, she began dolling herself up, as if getting ready for a date. Lip gloss brightened the pink in her lips. Brushing her long golden locks, she started flipping her hair to one side. Thanks to online tutorials, she was an expert at eyeshadow and decided to smoke-out her eyes so her blue eyes would pop. Her gray top made her skin tone pop just right against the white bathroom walls. With all of this coordinating, surely, she could take a decent picture.

That's it. Now the pose, need lots of eye play. Gotta bring the A game.

Pulling on a sleeve, she exposed a little of her shoulder and looked over her it in classic glamour shot allure. Happy with how she looked, she propped her phone, set the timer, and posed. *Click!* She had it.

She sent a Facebook message to DeeDee, her advocate in this venture and Sinder expert.

[Goldie: How's this for my profile shot? Is it ok?]

[DeeDee: Smokin'! But you need more photos. Full body shots. Show off those girls!]

[Goldie: Are you kidding me?]

[DeeDee: I thought you aimed to get fucked on V-day?]

Goldie's eyebrows lifted high. *She got me. That's the very least I wanted out of this. A bearded man with just the right dick to please me. All night long.*

[Goldie: What's your recommendation?]

[DeeDee: >:}~ A tight, little black dress, braless, and push out more cleavage, girl. Look like you're begging for that dick.]

[Goldie: Does the boss know you talk to our customers with that mouth?]

[DeeDee: Oh, he knows what else this mouth can do, afterhours and under his desk.]

[Goldie: OMG. You're a whore, DeeDee!!!!]

[DeeDee: And proud of it!]

Goldie dove into her closet. These days, she didn't have many dresses, but she never tossed the little black dress. With a slip, she weaseled the dress up and over, using the bathroom mirror as reference. Licking her cherry-flavored glossy lips, she juggled her thirty-two C-cup breasts together, the deep canyon of flesh made her appear more hour glassed. She pinched her nipples to keep them awake and alert.

Another round of timed photos and she sent them off to DeeDee for inspection.

[DeeDee: That's what I'm talking about! Now, post them all!]

Changing back into comfortable grey pajamas, she settled back on the couch. With a few gulps of her wine, she uploaded three photos: her glamour shot, a front body and side body shot. If they didn't want what she offered, then *fuck them.* Her glass empty, she refilled it, preparing for the questions she now needed to answer.

First question, what age range is she hunting for? *Let's keep them within ten years.*

Second question, gender preference? She hovered on *bisexual* for a moment before clicking *male. Sorry girls, I'm in the mood for a nice hard cock. Maybe next time.*

The questions were endless it seemed. From what her ideal date would be, to picking activities for outdoor and indoor. A standard marketing data collecting routine.

Did she like romantic comedies? *No. Though my life feels like one at this rate.*

Do I like to go dancing? *Uh, my experience is bumping and grinding at a crowded club. Does that count?*

Would you rather have steak, fish, or salad? *Depends. Who's buying? Ha!*

She refilled her glass, the heat of wine warming her cheeks. The time had come, to click FINISH. With this, the profile would be live, and she would be waiting for responses to roll in. No sooner had she refreshed the screen, she had thirty requests. *Well, at least I know the tan and makeup do work.* Blinking she sipped her wine and lifted and eyebrow. So many looked hot but lacked beards. She began swiping left for every bare faced man that hit her screen. Many came across the screen with long, short, and medium beards. She didn't care, she wanted them all.

Her imagination ran wild, drunk on wine as she poured the last of the bottle. The liquid courage now had her imagining one of these men between her legs, whether it was their beards or dicks didn't matter. Her pussy throbbed with want. Closing her eyes, she could imagine the tattooed biker man from first beard's profile towering over her. Peeking at his images once more, she could see the bare chest with a happy trail leading down to his pants.

The v-shaped bulge said it all, *he's packing.*

She swiped right. *Yes, please!*

I few swipes to the left brought her to the next eye candy, a serious, furrowed-brow man locking eyes with her. Another swirl and sip of her wine and her mind wondered back to the bottom of the gutter. *I need sex.* She could see him towering over her with that glare, pulling her hair and smacking her ass. Finishing her wine, she swiped right, hunting for at least one more.

After powering through, sliding left again and again, she paused on one. He didn't have sex appeal photos like the ones before, but he was handsome. Lifting an eyebrow, she wondered what hid under that loose t-shirt. The tattoos on his arms hinted to more art across his canvas. He had long wavy hair and a longer beard than the others, as if he were a casual mountain man.

Those hazel eyes sent a shudder through her. *Gawd he's sexy.*

Goldie's hand slid into her pajama pants, pushing her panties to the side. She flipped through his remaining photo, the muscles pulling on his clothes, muscular thighs, and shins. Closing her eyes, her finger dove between her pink folds, her swollen clit slick with her arousal. She imagined undressing him, imagining what those tattoos might look like, how far they painted his body, and how they rolled over his chiseled body.

Laying the phone to the side, her other hand glided under her pajama shirt and groped a bare breast. Twisting a nipple, her fingers dove back inside her pussy. *Oh, what I wouldn't give to have him play with me. All of me. To feel the heat of his mouth on my breasts, to feel that beard between my thighs.* Her fingers returned to circle her clit, her body arching as she squeezed her breast tighter. She peaked, moaning as she collapsed forward, opening her eyes at last.

She swiped right. *Good grief, maybe I need to add NSF to my profile.*

Her phone continued to buzz from Sinder notifications. It appeared beard one and beard two have already responded. Now to set up the dates.

The Guber Driver

Goldie slid into the back of her Guber and tilted her head. Her driver was a cute tattooed hunk. He even had a clean-cut short beard that made his chiseled jaw and pompadour haircut complement his overall look.

He turned to her, lifting an eyebrow as he eyed his cell phone for second. "Goldie, I presume?" His voice was smooth and suave as he addressed her.

Where was his profile on Sinder? "Yes, that's me." She buckled in, searching his hazel eyes. "And you're my Guber, yes?"

He sucked his bottom lip and nodded, turning to focus on driving as he put the vehicle into drive. She stared at him, something about him seemed strangely familiar, as if she'd seen him before. *Not from work or I would've recognized the voice.*

"Are you sure this is where you're going?" He broke the silence.

"That's the address he gave me." Glancing at her phone, she brought it up again. "*Red's Bar.*"

"Have you been there before?" He gave her a quick look through the rearview mirror.

Why the hell would he care? "N-no." Her face flushed, and she glared out the window.

"So, *he* picked it, huh?" Humming to himself, he continued prying further. "Was there some place you'd rather go?"

Is this his way of stealing another man's date? She smiled, shaking her head before meeting his gaze. "Shouldn't you watch the road instead, Mister..." She glanced down at the phone. "Charles."

"Come on. You can't tell me your idea for an outing with your boyfriend was a bar." He flipped the blinker and waited in the turn lane. "Just entertain me for a moment."

Oh, good grief. Why can't I just not reply? "I don't mind bar food," Goldie deflected.

Scoffing, the car turned, and he retorted. "But anyone can do bar food. Hell. Even chain restaurants with better wine selection have bar food."

Goldie opened her mouth to fight him on the matter, but she couldn't. *Dammit, he's got a point.*

"That dress and the way you carry yourself... I bet you're a red wine fan."

Normally, I'd be pissed. But coming from someone gorgeous and the way he said it, it's a bit of a turn on. She smirked. "You got me. And it's not a boyfriend. Just a first date."

"Oh?" He pulled next to a curb and parked. "Well, good luck on your date."

See you nosy-hot-Guber-driver!

Goldie stepped out of her Guber, standing in front of *Red's Bar* and froze. She had seen the good reviews online, but this evening, the parking lot was packed with motorcycles. Her phone buzzed with a message from her first beard, and she ignored it. Biting her lip, she had dressed in a tight little red slip-on dress, complete with matching red lingerie. She expected a hot date, not a party with a local biker gang.

The car window rolled down. "Hey. You ok?"

"Y-yes." She narrowed her eyes at him, feeling the weight of defeat. *Why does the Guber driver look familiar?*

"Are you sure this is the right address?" He questioned the locale and situation.

Putting on a brave smile, she spun on her heel. "Yea, looks like the right place. I just didn't expect a biker gang here too. Blind dates, ha." Her face flushed. *Shit-shit-shit. Why did I let that fact slip? He will think I'm a complete idiot.*

He furrowed his brow, giving her a skeptical smirk. "I can take you back home. Or elsewhere?"

Elsewhere? What is he planning? No. I will stick with the plan. My first beard is waiting for me.

She considered it for a good minute, then said, "No, I'll stay."

"Ok." He shrugged. "But, let me give you my number."

"What?" She leaned into the car window, lifting an eyebrow. "Why?"

He locked eyes with her. "No offense... uh...?" He lingered, searching for her name.

"Goldie."

"Look, Goldie. A pretty girl like you, walking into a bar full of bikers doesn't sit well with me." He scribbled his number on a sticky note. "Just keep this handy, if you ever need me. Tonight, or any other night."

"Do you do this for all the pretty girls?" She laughed, reading his name. "Chuckles? Really?"

"Nickname of mine." He winked. "And no. Only those I drop off at biker bars with no signs of their date waiting at the door."

She stuck her tongue out at him, and he laughed.

"Just, watch yourself in there."

"Yes, sir. See you around, Chuckles." Rolling her eyes, she pulled herself from the car.

"Same to you, Goldie."

With that Chuckles left her standing in the parking lot.

First Beard

The neon sign, reading *Red's Bar* overhead, buzzed. The rowdy crowd could be heard laughing and hollering within. Adjusting her purse strap, she couldn't help but regret leaving the pepper spray behind to make room for the condoms. *I only needed one. Not the whole fucking box. Shit, I look desperate.*

Her phone pinged, and she pulled it from her pocket.

[First Beard: You here?]

[Goldie: Yes. Just arrived.]

[First Beard: Come on in! Wat r u waiting 4?]

Scoffing, there it was. That annoying lazy text writing she loathed.

Gripping onto her purse strap for support, she marched through the worn wooden door. Inside, she was met with a cacophony of clacking pool balls, Molly Hatchett piercing over the crackling speakers, and shouts coming from the rowdy bikers. Blinking to adjust to the dim lighting and smoky ambience, she paled. They all wore the same biker gang vest, a local chapter of the *Outlaws* spread out before her and she groaned.

Like a deer walking into a den of hungry wolves, the atmosphere came to a screeching halt. The lyrics filled her ears, *we're flirtin' with disaster, ya'll know what I mean*. Smiles rippled across the gang's face, their hungry eyes picking her apart in a way that made her feel dirty and naked. *I didn't sign up for a gang bang.*

The biggest in the group with the older, tattered vest pushed through the core of the group. "Damn girl! You're hot!" A long-bearded man with salt and peppered hair pulled into a tight ponytail approached, loud and monstrous. "Goldie, right?"

Oh gawd, don't tell me this is him. "Y-yea." Panic filled her. *Asshole, you look nothing like your picture! Unkempt beard, much older, and a slight gut? Did you trade in your six pack for another version? What the fuck!* "And you're..." She glanced at her phone. "Tex? Is that short for something?"

A toothy grin shifted under the burly beard. "Besides being from Texas." He laid the accent on thick for this, puffing out his chest which did nothing to hide the gut. "You know what they say about Texas, don't ya?"

Oh no, this is not what I signed up for. This isn't what your Sinder profile had on it, Mr. Texas. Don't get me wrong, you are so much bigger in real life. But in all the wrong places.

"Everything's bigger in Texas. Including me." He groped his crouch, and Goldie swallowed, adverting her gaze. "Hope you came to party, girl. You look just like your pictures. I'm impressed. I can't wait to see if you're a natural blonde under that dress."

"Uh, excuse me. It was a long ride. Where's the bathroom?" *What fresh hell have I gotten into?*

"Right over there, baby doll." The group cleaved, forming a path to the door.

"Thank you." Goldie rushed into the restroom. Much to her surprise, it was halfway decent.

The bar had all the workings of a dive, but the ladies' room was on par with any night club she'd visited. She leaned on the counter, staring at her reflection in disbelief. Scrambling for her phone, she didn't know how to get herself out. The sticky note had come out, she shook her head and shoved it back in her purse. Her thumbs worked fast.

[Goldie: This is a shit show!!!!!!]

[DeeDee: What? You're not talking about First Beard????]

[Goldie: Yes, First Beard!]

23

A roar of laughter came through the door, and she cringed. She walked into a stall and flushed the toilet. At least, she had to make sure he knew she was using the bathroom. The anxiety of walking out there among the biker gang made every nerve tighten in her joints.

[Goldie: He's older, fatter, and he's a leader of a biker gang]

[DeeDee: WHAT?!]

[Goldie: I don't know what to do! HELP!]

She turned on the sink to buy her time. *DeeDee! Get me out of this!*

[DeeDee: Call the Guber back!]

[Goldie: I am not calling Chuckles!]

[DeeDee: Who the hell is Chuckles???]

The door swung open and Goldie shoved her phone into the purse. A toothy grin spread on Tex's face as he waltzed into the restroom. Eyes wide, Goldie gave him a baffled expression and tilted her head. He closed the door, the men outside whistling, cheering him on.

The door shut, and he locked it behind him, then leaned against it. She was trapped.

He licked his upper teeth, his hungry eyes roving over her, from head to toe, then back again. "I imagine you reached out to me on Sinder, wanting a little more Texas in you."

And it's clear you only responded for the chance for sex. "You just get right down to the point. I was hoping for a real date," she said, afraid to move closer to him.

"Oh, but baby doll, you have me hard already." Like an unsolicited dick pic, he unzipped, and the biggest cock Goldie had ever seen stood at attention.

And now my curiosity is overwriting my logic. "I'm about to go through the big D." Goldie muttered, her eyes unable to break her stare on the huge cock, her loins aching with want. *It's been weeks. No, since what? December? And Valentine's day tomorrow. This may have been a dud, but how can I say no to a chance to ride a dick built like a train car? Fuck it, let's do this. He's got a Dadbod. There's nothing wrong with that.* "So, we're just hooking up for the sex today, huh?"

25

"Thought that was the plan." He winked and gave her a smirk.

Goldie had to give him some credit. He didn't dare move a muscle from the door, there had been some sort of moral code mixed in with the blatant passes to just fuck. Raising an eyebrow, she didn't bring lube. Surely a dick the size of a giant dildo would need lube, or she'd have to be wet as hell to make this work. She glanced into her open purse. Damn. *These condoms won't fit that monster cock.*

"You got condoms for that weapon?"

"Fuck ya, I do." Out of his back pocket he produced a Magnum XL. And without further ado, rolled it on.

He closed the gap between them, butterflies in Goldie's stomach as the large dick became ever more intimidating. The heat of his hands pulled her dress up over her hip, fingers hooking her lacy underwear and tugging them down. Red lace fell down her shins, over her ankles and over heeled toes.

Tex gripped her, picking her up and propping her on the counter. "You know what blondes and noodle have in common?" His beard tickled at her neck, lips at her ear.

"No?" Goldie wasn't sure if he was trying to be clever or tell a cheesy bar joke. *Oh my God, he sucks at talking on all levels. Just when my libido was starting to heat up.*

"They both wiggle when you eat'em."

Before she could absorb what exactly he said, he had knelt and pressed his lips to her clit. He suckled, his beard tickling her pussy and inner thigh. She leaned back, propping herself on the counter as she spread her leg s wider. The back of her head pressed against the mirror and she closed her eyes, indulging in the pleasure buzzing through her body.

The heat of his tongue teased the opening of her vagina before twirling around her clit once more. She moaned, goosebumps making her body shudder. There was nothing she loved more than the sensation of a bearded man eating her out. He had a long beard, and it

27

wasn't the preferred length for her pleasure, but it beat a bare faced man. Hands-down. Again, his tongue teased her opening, and fingers dove inside. She arched, knees hugging his shoulders, jittering with the electricity of her arousal.

With one hard pull on her clit, he made her shriek. The fingers rode hard and deep, her wetness flowing from her as she began to orgasm. His lips released and she reached down to grip his hair, to demand more of his oral pleasuring.

He smacked her hand from his hair. "Don't touch the tail, sweetie."

Shut up! You're killing my libido again!

It was a sobering cold shower on the moment. She blinked, panting as he stood to fix his hair in the mirror over her shoulder. *Note to self. Don't let this man speak or I won't get off a second time.* His cock rubbed against her swollen clit, and her heart leapt into her throat. *Shit he's big. Will it fit? I can't back down now, can I?*

"Shame we ain't got any lube-"

Goldie pressed her fingers against his lips. "No more talking, just fucking." *I can't take another comment of belligerent biker dialogue.*

The tip of his ginormous cock pressed against her opening. She stiffened and they glared at each other, gauging the reaction as he pressed further, slow and calculating. DeeDee had made fun of her huge dildo once, but it couldn't have prepared her for this. The tip pressed further in, the hard cock like a police baton. Her loins ached in a new way with no room for tensing and squeezing.

She wiggled, calming herself, relaxing on par to being amid a gynecology exam. "Dammit your big," she breathed as he slid a little further in, making her fight the need to tense.

"I'll go slow, baby doll." His hands slid across atop her thighs. "Mmm, you're so tight."

Who wouldn't be! You're fucking half-horse with a dick this size!

As he rode deeper inside, he at last hit a spot that made her feel like he was knocking on her belly button. He wasn't even all the way

29

in but was very aware this was the end of the line for the Texas Express Train. A hand glided between thin, his thumb rubbing her clit. The waves of pleasure were only met with the brick wall of the agonizing inability to squeeze. It was like over stretching a hamstring or bicep.

He began a slow rocking, his dick sliding slowly in and out, gaining more range with each pass. Goldie was in turmoil, pleasure and discomfort mangling through her. She wanted more, and on the other hand, wanted it to end. Tex started to moan, and she secretly sung the praises to whatever guardian looked over her. She relaxed and at last, enjoyed the slow pace as he grinded against her gently.

Bigger dick isn't the best fit, but at least I'm starting to enjoy this!

Tex gripped the side of the counter, shoving in hard one last time as he came. Goldie yelped, convinced her belly button had popped or at least knocked on her cervical door. It was painful and relief filled her as he left her body. She sat there, head leaning on the mirror wondering, what the hell made her think this was a great idea?

Shit. Talk about ruining my climax yet again!

"You need a ride home?" He pulled the condom off and flung it into the trash can.

She sighed. "No, I'll call a Guber."

"You ok, baby doll?" One sink over, he began washing his face and beard as she slid off the counter, wiggling her underwear back on.

"You've ruined me, Tex," she confessed. "Bigger isn't better."

He snorted, drying his face. "But you were so good, sweetheart."

She gave him an unamused glare, and he laughed.

"You could have said something, darling." He unlocked the door and paused. "I didn't make you feel pressured?" His voice had abandoned the rough-n-tough biker tone and softened.

"No, no..." Goldie sighed, pushing into the bathroom stall. "I was too curious. And

31

honestly, I was searching for sex. No offense, Tex, but I didn't realize that some part of me wanted a real date after all."

He snorted. "But trust me, girlie. No man wants a girl not enjoying herself. Next time speak up. And if he takes offense, he's an asshole and you call old Tex to come take care of them."

"Uh, I wasn't expecting a favor from a biker gang out of this." She laughed from her porcelain throne.

GUBER HOME

Reluctant, Goldie made her way back through the bar. This first date had so much promise, but in the end, Texas was too big for even her appetite.

Sighing, she hit the app. The Guber would be here in a matter of minutes. *How lucky could I get?*

Tex winked at her as she pushed through the doors. The sun had started to set, and a familiar car pulled to the curb, exactly where she had been dropped off. Looking to her phone, the message flipped to, *your driver has arrived.* Then she saw it. *Driver name: Charles. Chuckles didn't leave. Was he waiting for me? Are you kidding me?*

Furrowing her brow, she marched to the car as he rolled the window down. Leaning in, she narrowed her eyes at him. In turn, he raised his own and lowered the music.

After a minute of gauging silence, he tilted his head. "Need a ride?"

No shit, I pinged on Guber and you pulled up. Of course, I need a ride! "Did you even leave?" she blurted. "Chuckles."

He gave a toothy grin, scratching at his beard. "I took a lunch break nearby."

Bullshit! "Thanks for the vote of confidence." Her face reddened, embarrassed and frustrated. *He knew I wouldn't call him. But I don't mind being chauffeured by someone this handsome.*

"Look, if it makes you feel better, you stayed longer than I thought." The confession did nothing for relieving her heated cheeks. "You want to sit up front?" He patted the seat

She snorted, then smirked. "No. I'll sit in the back," she said, wondering if his hand would snake up her thigh if she had taken the offer. *No, Goldie. You still have one more date and possibly a third if beard three ever replies. I wish Sinder showed if someone read the damn message.*

She slid into the car, pulled out her phone and opened the app.

"Home or... somewhere else?" He patiently stared at her through the mirror.

"Like your place?" Goldie lifted an eyebrow, reading DeeDee's text.

[DeeDee: What the hell happened? DO YOU NEED HELP! Answer your text, woman!]

He leaned over the seat, demanding her eyes, but she ignored him.

[Goldie: He had a dick the size of a nightstick! Too fucking big! And now the Guber driver is hitting on me!!]

"Are you fucking with me?" His voice came out low, and she met his gaze.

"You are serious." Goldie's heart raced. "We just met."

"I'm not the one with a box of condoms meeting bikers in dive bars." He pointed at the seat beside her. Laughing, he continued his observations, "And it's quite intimidating to see a box with my name and number stuck to it."

Mortified, she grabbed the sticky note and shoved it into her purse. The chuckling rolling from him agonizing. *Now I know where he got the nickname from.*

"Seriously. I'll take you anywhere you want." He turned away, cancelling the Guber ride. "This one's on me for being a dick. Home, right?"

Biting her lip, Goldie looked to her phone.

[DeeDee: Was first beard hot? Is Guber guy hot? What is happening?!]

[Goldie: First beard was Dadbod. But had a dick fit for a horse!]

[DeeDee: Ok... not a complete lost. Wait, was that Chuckles?]

Looking back up, her breath caught in her throat, locking gazes with his hazel stare. "Take your time. We're not on the clock now. Car's in park. I'll wait."

[Goldie: Chuckles is the Guber driver.]

[DeeDee: And??????]

"Hey, Chuckles?" He twisted back around, and she snapped a photo of him.

"Ok...?" Tilting his head. "You think I plan on kidnapping you or something?" Her silence pleaded the fifth and he snorted. "At least let me pose for the shot."

"Fine." She raised her phone once more. "Ready?"

He wiggled further into view, his broad chest and shoulders visible. "Ready."

She lifted her thumb and as she pressed, he shifted his pose. Lifting his shirt, the ripples of his abs sent a hot wave of arousal over her. His pierced tongue had protruded forward, and he had lifted his eyebrow. Goldie stared at the image. *Would it be wrong to use this as masturbating material later? My gawd he's hot and...* She hit send. The image now in of DeeDee's possession for final judgment.

"Did it turn out ok?" He settled back into his driver seat, pulling on his seat belt.

[DeeDee: Why aren't you fucking Guber Driver Dude!!!]

"Oh, it did." She sucked on her inner cheek. "Your girlfriend must be lucky."

He made a clicking sound with his mouth. *Was that him clacking his piercing on his teeth?*

The car started moving forward and *Red's Bar* disappeared on the horizon. It grew dark outside, the streetlamps fading in and out of the car window.

At last, Goldie asked, "What was that reaction for? When I asked about a girlfriend?" *Now it's my turn to ask personal questions.*

"No girlfriend. She left me for another guy because I didn't spend all my money on her." The car slowed and came to a complete stop, the traffic thick and unmoving. "Ugh, I forgot there's a big concert tonight. I should have gone the other way." He put the car into park.

"You can't just put the car in park while in traffic?" Goldie protested.

"Look, the last time this happened, I didn't move for thirty minutes. Now's a good time to check emails and watch shows on your phone." He pulled out his phone, suddenly disinterested, as if mentioning a girlfriend had spoiled the mood.

I ruined what could have been a good time. Goldie looked to her phone, a message from Second Beard flashing in her notifications, confirming the address and time for their date tomorrow. *Goal achieved. I've got a date for Valentine's Day.*

Flipping through, she pulled up the non-responsive Third Beard's profile. *He looks so damn familiar.* Looking at Chuckles, he was still playing on his phone. The car had stopped under a dark area and traffic hadn't budged an inch.

Let's send another message.

[Goldie: Hi, C.J. I was wondering if you received my first message.]

Uh, I sound desperate. She pulled up the picture of Chuckles, biting her lip as she

39

wiggled in her seat. Tex had felt good in the end but she just didn't feel... satisfied. Her pussy wet, her arousal waving through her. Another stolen glance and Chuckles furrowed his brow as he paid attention to his phone, not her. She gauged the darkness between them. *If I'm quiet, maybe I can...*

Holding her phone in one hand, the other snaked up her inner thigh. Another stolen glance and she was satisfied Chuckles wouldn't even know what fun she would incur in his back seat. Pushing the lacy red underwear out of the way, she began circling her clit, slow and steady.

[Third Beard: Are you available tomorrow night?]

She paused her activities, responding as she slid her thumb across the keyboard.

[Goldie: I have another arrangement at two.]

[Third Beard: Let me convince you to spend Valentine's Day with me.]

Aren't we a bold one? She smirked, returning to playing with herself as she replied.

[Goldie: How about a round of sexting? Give me a preview of how we might end the night?]

DeeDee would be proud of me for this one, ha!

[Third Beard: Ok. I'll play along. You've already got me hard. Tell me, how wet does my picture make you?]

Cheeky!

[Goldie: I grab your hand and slide it up my thigh, letting you feel how slick I am.]

[Third Beard: Leaning in, I whisper in your ear, "I want to watch you come" as I start to circle your clit.]

[Goldie: I moan, your beard tickling my neck. My hands slide down your torso, pulling at your pants. Please show me your cock, baby.]

Chuckles shifted in the driver seat, and Goldie froze. She had forgotten she was still in his car. He pulled it out of park and moved up a car length and parked again. Never once looking her way, returning to his phone. Whatever he was doing, he didn't want to stop playing as his thumbs slide over the screen.

41

[Third Beard: I help you unbutton my jeans, and I moan as the heat of your fingers wrap around my hard cock.]

[Goldie: I begin rubbing your hardon, opening my legs wider.]

[Third Beard: My fingers slide into your pussy, stroking in and out. You're so wet my cock throbs in your hands.]

She slid her own fingers between her pink folds. Enjoying the imagery he painted, her head tilted back eyes closed. She thrusted in and out of herself, growing more wet with each rotation. Through heavy-lidded eyes, she slid her message, her wish to him

[Goldie: Faster. Please stroke faster.]

[Three Beard: I want to taste you on my lips.]

Goldie lurched forward, her orgasm taking her breath away. She bit her tongue, silencing the moan she would have released if it weren't for–her gaze met hazel eyes in the mirror, and her heart stopped. Panting, the orgasm still sent shiver across her body as she pulled her dress back over her thighs.

"Feel better? Not every day my passenger gets their rocks off sexting in my back seat." Chuckles spoke with intrigue in his voice, a mischievous smirk on his face. "And here I thought I was sexually frustrated."

"You're a creep for watching." Goldie looked away, despair swallowing her up.

"What was I supposed to do?" Frustration filled his voice. "Reach back there and play out what you were sending?" He twisted, raising a brow. "I don't know about you, but it's been a few months since I hooked up with anyone. And you're making this an exceedingly difficult ride."

Goldie paled. "I'm sorry. It's been since December for me and…" At last she wavered and looked back to him. He narrowed his eyes at her, the clicking of his tongue piercing making her shift in her seat. *What would that feel like rolling over…* "I am beyond frustrated.

Hot and bothered and not getting what I want," she blurted, much to her own surprise.

"I see that." His eyes studied her, *all* of her. He bit his bottom lip, weighing his next words.

Goldie's heart raced. *Am I about to fuck my Guber driver? Am I really that horny to open myself to any invitation? At least Chuckles seems to care...*

A car horn filled the air, ruining the moment. Traffic had started moving again and for the remainder of the ride, they remained silent. The streetlights only fueled her curiosity.

She looked down at her phone.

[Goldie: Thanks for the good time. Maybe I will call you tomorrow.]

Nothing. Third beard had disappeared as fast as he had made her come.

6

NEVER GONNA GIVE YOU UP

[Second Beard: Are you here yet?]

Goldie scoffed. *How impatient. I'm only fifteen minutes away. We agreed to meet at two, not one-thirty, buddy.*

The Guber app had given her a few riders, but she had refused them all. She needed to see Chuckles, apologize, or make amends. All night she had tossed and turned. His picture haunting her, and she cursed under her breath. *Why the hell didn't I hook up with Chuckles! The man wanted to. Hell, I wanted to!*

She dug into her purse, then paused. The box of condoms was there, and the sticky note still stuck attached. She cancelled driver after driver. *Dammit, Chuckles. You're going to make me do it.* She punched in his phone number and saved it. Inhaling deep, she began typing the message. She wanted this in writing, not as a call where her panic would force her to hang up on him. *I've done that before. Never heard from that guy again. Let's not completely blow this.*

[Goldie: Hey Chuckles, you working tonight?–Goldie]

She waited, tugging on her slip-on black dress. She had decided to wear the teaser dress with the bra and underwear. She had settled with the idea DeeDee's instructions had led her down the way of one-night stands. Granted, she had failed to make it clear whether or not she was aiming for sex or a date. Who knew what tonight would hold for her? Tex had been upfront and to the point. Maybe Second

Beard would want something more. *Or I'm daydreaming.*

The message to Chuckles shifted from *delivered* to *read*. Nothing happened, no signs of him writing. She couldn't stand it. Biting her lip, she thought for a moment. *I will not be ignored!*

[Goldie: Look, yesterday I was a hot mess. I'm sorry. Desperate for a date on Valentine's day. I know, stupid right? C'mon, I had a blind date with a biker and still didn't back down, so you already know I can't make good judgment calls.] She paused and smiled to herself. [What I do know is you're the best damn Guber driver, and I trust you to save me if this blind date goes South tonight.]

Closing her eyes, she sighed in relief. It was done, she let the truth out. *I sound like a fucking moron.*

Her phone buzzed.

[Chuckles: Did you just friend zone me?]

Her jaw fell slack. *Why can't I do anything like a normal human being?!* Sinking to her

47

knees, she wanted to cry. *Great job, now you've definitely slammed and locked that door tight and threw out the–*

A honk from a car made her lose balance, and she fell back onto the sidewalk. The window on a familiar white car rolled down. She couldn't contain her excitement. Her phone pinged; *driver has arrived.* Scrambling to her feet, she snatched up her purse and slide into the front passenger seat.

"Did you seriously just friend zone me for watching? I'm a man, what did you think I would do?" He scowled at her.

"No!" She pulled on the seatbelt. "Look, I just, I already made plans with this guy before I met you and I feel...obligated."

"Valentine's Day," he blurted. "Just one other guy, huh?"

"I doubt this will work out," she confessed, her gut uneasy by the Second Beard's impatient vibe. "And the third guy..."

"Third guy?" The car was travelling towards their destination. "Did you just message every guy on Sinder after downing a bottle of wine?"

Her eyes widened and looked away.

"You didn't!" he cackled.

"I'm so glad you're amused by this." *Asshole.*

"And did you just deny every Guber driver waiting for me?" She spun her head back as he made the next turn. "If so, I can't say that some part of mine finds that kind of cute and attractive."

"I just don't want you to think I'm... easy." Blushing she turned to the window again, enjoying the safety of staring at his reflection through the glass.

"Oh, that box of condoms totally didn't help that impression." Sighing, he glanced down at the GPS. "Looks like we're here. Be safe. You have my number, so..."

"Right." They stared into each other's eyes for a moment. "I'm leaving now."

"I know." He gave her a baffled look. "At least this is some high-end luxury apartments. Hope you have a better time."

Clearing her throat, she opened the door. "T-thanks."

SECOND BEARD

After being buzzed in, the idea of ditching the blind date had vanished. Whoever she was about to hook-up with had money, and good taste. She wondered the halls, isolated in the silence of marble flooring and six panel doors with golden numbers and keycode pads.

She glanced at her phone.

[Goldie: I'm here.]

[Second Beard: 140]

Snorting, she hoped the vague response was the room number. At least, Tex had more manners, meeting her at the door. Searching for his Sinder profile, he wasn't bad looking and had an impressive profile. *John. What a boring name.*

At last, she found the room and knocked. It took a few minutes, and he opened the door.

Goldie's breath caught. He was gorgeous, dark haired with blue eyes, and... *where the hell is his beard? Did he shave it off! What a complete sham! Calm down, no fair to him if I just end the date on that note. I can salvage this.* She imagined him taller when she first seen his images, but again, that was through a haze of wine.

He motioned for her to come in, smiling, hunger in his eyes. A shudder rocked her shoulders as she passed the threshold. Inside, she discovered minimalistic postmodern décor and furniture. Her eyes scanned the kitchen and tall dining room table, and her gut twisted. *Where are the candles? The flowers or even... dinner? Maybe we're going out to eat?*

She recovered her smile and spun to face John as he closed the door. His shirt laid open and unbutton. As he took long strides across the black tiles, he began to unbuckle his belt. Goldie's body took several strides backwards until she locked knees on the couch and sat down.

"Uh, whoa there." She searched for words. *Words would be good right about now!* "John? John, I thought maybe..."

"Feel it, it's already hard," he said, low and breathy as he towered over her.

"Wait, what?" Goldie shook her eyes. *This man is beyond impatient.*

"Here." He gripped her wrist and shoved it on his crotch. "It wants you."

Blinking, she squeezed and rubbed and... *where the hell is it?*

"Yea, squeeze me a little harder. Just like that, baby," he cooed, tilting his hip towards her, eyes closed.

Jerking her hand away, she ducked to the side of him, fleeing the couch. *NOPE! I'm not going to even try. Not after Tex. I just want a normal sized dick, and this guy has failed.* She started for the door, but he grabbed her arm. Glaring down at his hand, she at last looked up into angry face.

She frowned. "Look, I didn't..."

He unzipped his pants and revealed his... *What is that? An elevator button? A mole? A... NOPE! Definitely not getting any satisfaction with bad impression on top of it. I mean, you can't be a douchebag and have a small dick. That's not attractive.* She tried to leave again, but he squeezed her arm tighter. "Where do you think you're going?" he asked. "You promised me a good time." A wicked grin came across his bare face, and he let go. "Come on, baby. I thought you wanted to hook up with me, with this." He motioned to himself, and she paled. "You can't leave now?"

Come on. Think, think. This asshole won't let me go unless he gets something out of me and... "I was gonna get my friend." Her mind spun, cooking up a half assed plan.

"Oh? She wants to join us?"

Of course, you think I meant another female.

Fine, I can work with that. "You know, I'll just call her and tell her to head over. Where's the bathroom? Just want to freshen up, you know?"

"Sure, sure, baby doll." He motioned to a room on the exterior side. "What's your friend's name, sweetheart?"

He followed her to the bathroom, and she practically slammed the door in his face, locking it. "Uh, her name?" Goldie looked around the bathroom. The small window by the tub looked like a tight squeeze. "She prefers nicknames in these situations." She turned on the sink faucet, hoping it would drown out the sound of her climbing into the tub and opening the window. *Thank God, he lives on the bottom floor!*

"Oh? What's that?" The knob wiggled and stopped.

CREEPER! Goldie unlocked the window latch and pushed up, opening with ease. "Uh, Tex. Her name's Tex!" *Oh! Where's my purse and phone! Tex did say if I needed him...*

"Why Tex?" He sounded unsure.

"Everything's bigger in Texas," she answered, texting the biker, then shoving her purse strap over her head and shoulder. With his address, the apartment number, and creeper – He'd know enough to throat punch John on her behalf.

"How so?" he asked flatly.

"Double D's, John. DOUBLE," she blurted, pushing the screen off and throwing her heels out the open window. "DOUBLE D's! You ever seen that?" *Double the dick of a normal man!*

"N-no. So, she's a busty girl like Dolly Parton, huh?"

Goldie made a disgusted face. "Sure. If that's what you like?" She teetered on the tub, starting to pull herself through the window.

The sound of motorcycles rumbling was a blessing. She squirmed with more urgency. The sound of a cell phone came through the bathroom door. The wiggling doorknob stopped. He muffled something, and she imagined it meant someone was buzzing to come into the building. *Tex is gonna be all sorts bigger than you expected, buddy.*

Her hips made it pass the windowsill, and she slid out with alarming speed. The ripping of fabric made her breath catch. On her left side, the seam popped open, thread and fabric fraying all the way up to under her arm, stopping at the cross-stitch.

She heard shouting in the room, and she scrambled for her phone.

[Tex: You ok? Where are you?]

[Goldie: Bolted out the bathroom window]

[Tex: Good girl. We'll teach this creeper a lesson. Did he hurt you?]

[Goldie: No. But it wasn't like I wanted to end the date so soon. Scared me.]

Another squeal echoed through the bathroom window, and she cringed.

[Tex: Get yourself home, girl. We got you.]

She stood and realized she only had one shoe. *Fuck it. I can buy shoes.*

THE MISSING
THIRD BEARD

Holding her dress together, she pinged for a Guber driver. Like she expected, Charles snatched her up. She rounded the corner of the apartments, and her phone pinged. Third Beard C.J. had responded. She kept walking toward the front of the building, where Chuckles had dropped her off. Opening the message, she decided she would turn him down. Sinder had just brought her one shit show after another. *No more. Horribly advice at this rate.*

[Third Beard: Is your date going ok?]

Freezing, she glared at the message and scrolled up. *I never said it was a date.*

[Goldie: How did you know that's what it was?]

[Third Beard: You told me.]

Scoffing, she marched with renewed vigor, crossing the front grassy area of the apartments.

[Goldie: I did not.]

[Third Beard: That bad? Is that why you needed a ride so soon again?]

Her heart skipped a beat. *What the fuck?*

[Third Beard: Look up, I brought you flowers.]

Baffled, her head jerked up.

"But I don't think these roses can fix your dress." Chuckles furrowed his brow, taking in her haphazard state. "What the hell happened and why..."

"You!" She glared at her phone and back up again. "The sexting yesterday! That too!"

He shrugged, puffing out his cheeks. "To be fair, I hadn't checked my Sinder profile until you dropped the girlfriend comment, and I

59

recognized you immediately. Thought it was a chance to make a move, but it backfired."

"But your profile picture." She stomped up to him, failing to keep her dress closed. "You look nothing like that!"

"The tattoos don't change." He scratched his beard. "I didn't care for the long hair and beard. Plus, no one wants to ride in a Guber if the driver looks like he just climbed down from the mountains."

Her lips parted, her thought snagging a moment before she conceded, "Yea, you have a point there."

"Let me ask this again." He cleared his throat. "Are you available tonight?"

Goldie looked to the dozen roses. "Yea, for you I am."

"Then get in the car before a hard breeze rips the rest of your dress off." He opened the front passenger door. "W-where's your shoes?"

She gave him a silencing stare, and he didn't dare press the question further. Once she settled in, he shut the door, tossing the bouquet in the back seat and cancelled her Guber. He checked his mirrors and pulled away from the nightmare second blind date. When it all faded into the bleak night, Goldie relaxed. She covered her face with her hands, some part of her glad she had escaped a terrible situation.

A chill rattled through her as the split seam opened wider. The car's air conditioning icy against her skin, but she didn't want to bother holding the damn thing closed any more. Steady breaths, she recalled yesterday in her mind. *When he grunted, I thought he was moving the car but it's because he was getting hard, wanted more, and...*

Through her hands she spoke, "What do I call you?"

"Call me?" The car took a turn and started down a curvy road.

"C.J.? Charles? Chuckles?"

"I go by all three." He laughed. "Chuckles is fine. But if that's too formal, C.J. works."

"Where are we going?" She pulled her hands from her face, looking at the passing streets.

"I figured you'd be hungry, so I'm treating you out." He smirked, and the car took another turn.

"Um, I hate to tell you this, C.J." Goldie squinted at him. "My dress ripped, and I'm half-naked."

"Oh, I know." He gave a toothy grin, a tattooed arm reaching over. His hand hot as it slid over her stomach and down her thigh before gliding up to grip her inner thigh. *A little further up and he'll...* "It's a dinner for two. I'm cooking."

"Cooking?" A heat washed over her as his hand continued squeezing and exploring, weaseling under her black lacy underwear. *A little further, please don't stop.* "You cook?"

"Yea, and few other things." His finger caressed her clit, and her breath caught. "Should I stop?"

"No." She cupped his hand, urging him to keep going. "Just don't wreck the car."

He scoffed, a smirk across his face. "You have no idea how badly I wanted to reach back and do this yesterday." His fingers dove into her pussy and she hummed. "How much I wanted to give you the very thing your sexts had desired."

"If I had–" Another gasp interjected as he shifted his angle. Her pussy tightened on his fingers as he stroked in and out.

"What was that?" He teased, the car slowing as they pulled into a closed restaurant parking lot. "If I had what?"

"Told me." She moaned, opening her legs wider as she fumbled for the lever to lay her seat back. "If you had said something about Sinder... Mmm."

The seat fell back and allowed him a moment to pull away from her, putting the car in park and cut the engine. His seatbelt flew off, and before she knew it, he leaned over her. The heat of his hands sent her heart racing. One flowed across her ribs, sliding under the lacy bra and squeezed her breast. The other rode over her hip and snaked under the front of her panties. His finger circled her clit and she arched.

"Tell me what you want."

His voice barely beat the fog of pleasure rolling through her. The fingers dipped into her, she tightened and her retreated, returning slick as he rolled over her swollen clit. Goldie moaned and he groped her breast tight in reply.

"I want you..." Her hands pushed his down, and he let her guide his fingers back inside her wet heat. "...to make me come again."

Shoving her dress open further, he shoved her bra off her breast and lowered his lips to her nipple. The tip of his tongue circled the firm nub, slow and teasing as his fingers began rubbing and stroking. She propped one leg onto the dashboard, giving him access to thrust deeper as she shivered with pleasure. Her breath quickened, blood rushing with heat and passion.

The knock of his tongue piercing came like an erotic electric shock.

She whimpered, and she lurched forward, only for him to push her back into the seat, still suckling her breasts. Her orgasm exploded, only egging him to stroke faster. Squealing, her body arched, and a gush of wet heat released. With a pop, he pulled away from her and left her alone in the car to catch her breath.

JUST RIGHT

Goldie had pulled the seat up right, wondering where C.J. had vanished to when her car door opened. With practiced motion, he had eased her out, kicking the car door shut and carried her into the old diner. Hugging onto his neck as he shoved through the doorway. Goldie looked all around, the remains of a 24-hour diner half tarped in renovations surrounded them. He didn't stop in the rows of booths and tables, passing through an opening in the bar top. They were now traversing a super clean, upgraded kitchen area. The restaurant may not have been ready to serve customers, but it was ready to cook anything you could throw at it.

"Where are you taking me?" She couldn't stop her heart from fluttering against her chest like a caged bird. "Why here?"

"I'm taking you to my bed." He had a serious look on his face, making his beard and jaw breathtaking in the dim lighting.

"Bed?" *Did he mistake the diner for his house?*

Pushing through the manager's door, as promised a bed filled one corner. He sat her down as gentle as he had lifted her out of the car. Turning away, Goldie watched the muscles in his back stretch and twist as he pulled off his shirt and began unbuckling his belt. *We're about to fuck, and something tells me everything is going to be just right.* Spurred by his motions, she wiggled her panties off and unlatched her bra. Frustration filled her as the hooks caught on the frayed edge of the ripped dress.

Muttering profanities under breath, she twisted, trying to reach behind her to untangle it. Strong hands came to the rescue, ripping the cross-stitch and with it, freeing her of the dress and bra. Her lips parted to thank him but found his pressing hard, hot, and hungry. Deepening her kiss, she wanted to find the object that had fascinated her about him in that picture from the car. Her tongue slid across the horizon of flesh, searching. The tip of her tongue flicked the piercing, and he moaned into her mouth.

The bed creaked as she let herself layback into nest of bedding, the comforter balled up behind her, making her back arch. His naked body hot between her thighs, his cock hard as he pressed it against her pussy, daring to enter her. She panicked. Pushing him back, he let her and gave her a wide-eyed expression.

"Condoms!"

He laughed. "I wasn't getting to that part yet. Can't a guy have fun first?"

She glared at him, unamused. "Condoms or nothing."

He stood to his feet and sashayed across the poorly lit room. The light bounced off his muscled body, the tattoos distorting the shadows and curves, making his bare skin more pronounced as it trailed down to between his thighs. He rolled the condom onto his erection, nowhere near the size of Texas, but damn, it made her ache to have him. As he closed the gap between them, she balled the sheets in her fist, spreading herself to receive him.

C.J. knelt before her, his arms wrapping around her thighs, tugging her to the edge of the bed. His tongue licked across her pussy and when his tongue piercing connected with her clit, she came alive. The beard tickled and raked her skin. Chills rippled across her, the sensation provocative and goading her lust to have more of him. Her thighs fought to flee the overwhelming euphoria as he circled and flicked the tender swollen jewel. Goldie's fingers tangled in his hair, wanting more, scared of the orgasm building at alarming speed. The hardened muscles in his arms only added to the arousal consuming her body and soul.

Goldie peaked. The cry visceral as she

bowed. It was short lived as his lips locked wither her, muffling it. His cock slid in, hard as she throbbed and tightened. Her orgasm still rolled through her as he began grinding against her. The heat of his body weighed over her, her breast pressing against his torso, his arms wrapping under her. Her thighs tightened around him, rising her knees, letting him deeper into her.

He deepened the kiss before pulling away, panting against her neck. "You feel so good. It's hard to hold back."

"A little more." She let go of the sheets, her fingers clawing at his back. "Don't stop."

He grunted, a hand gliding down to her lower back and arching. His back bowed, moaning. She could feel him throb inside her. He pressed his hip against hers, grinding deep against her as he came. Her legs shook and toes curled. At last, she let go, allowing herself to rest in his arms. He slowed until he stopped, still inside her. Pulling away, he looked down at her and pulled a strand of hair from her face. Her lips curved into a smile as her breathing slowed.

"You seem satisfied." He smirked, pushing against her. "How was it?"

Meeting his gaze, she confessed, "Just right. But now, I'm hungry."

He hung his head in defeat. "I'm out of eggs, but I did make some porridge. You game?"

"As long as its not too hot, and not too cold."

THE END

HONEY CUMMINGS

A passionate, award-winning author of Fantasy, Honey has turned her aim toward erotica. Blending everyday scenarios, and crafting them into steamy, blood-boiling moments for every shade of audience. Whether you want something short and hot, like a student-teacher hook up to the more paranormal flair, where Sleep with Sasquatch has unexpected bonus, look forward to erotic short stories, novellas, and hopefully a Trilogy in the future. Honey's debut erotic short landed at No. 3 in Urban Erotica and continues to satisfy readers time and time again. Be sure to leave her a review and let her know what you think!

FOLLOW HONEY CUMMINGS

amazon.com/Honey-Cummings/e/
B07WFX5FDX

AuthorHoneyCummings.com

instagram.com/authorhoneycummings

twitter.com/HoneyCummings2

facebook.com/Author-Honey-
Cummings-101408818012749

MORE HONEY CUMMINGS BOOKS

Writing as Valerie Willis

Cedric: The
Demonic Knight
Romasanta: Father of
Werewolves
The Oracle: Keeper of the
Gaea's Gate
Artemis: Eye of Gaea
King Incubus:
A New Reign

Queen Succubus: Holder
of the Crown
Val's House of Musings: A
Mixed Genre Short Story
Collection

Writer's Bane:
Research 101
Writer's Bane: Formatting

Writing MM Romance as VC Willis

The Prince's Priest
The Priest's Assassin
The Assassin's Saint

The Champion's Lord: YONDER webnovel
Champion's Love: KU short story

MORE EROTICA BOOKS FROM 4 HORSEMEN PUBLICATIONS

LGBT Erotica

DISCOVER MORE AT
4HORSEMENPUBLICATIONS.COM

www.ingramcontent.com/pod-product-compliance
Lightning Source LLC
Chambersburg PA
CBHW030221130726
47898CB00013B/1041